Check also out the other Books by @hannasroth:

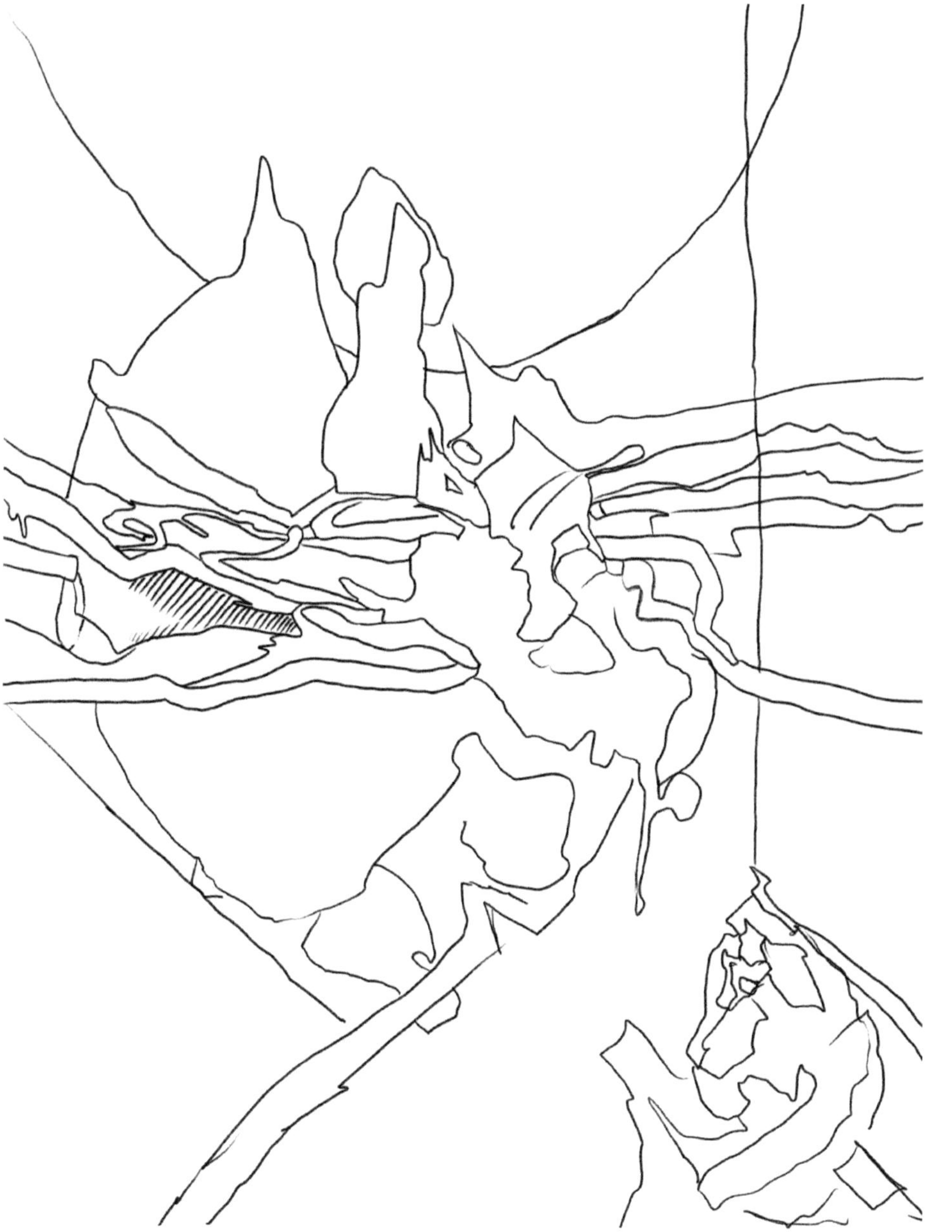

"Abstract-Coloring-Book"

Check also out the other Books by @hannasroth:

"Animal-ABC-Coloring-Book"

Check also out the other Books by @hannasroth:

"Reimagining Art: A Coloring
Book of Timeless Treasures"

Check also out the other Books by @hannasroth:

"Fridge Notes:
Liebesbotschaften"

Check also out the other Books by @hannasroth:

"Looking for (lovely) Monsters"
A creativity-enhancing-coloring-book

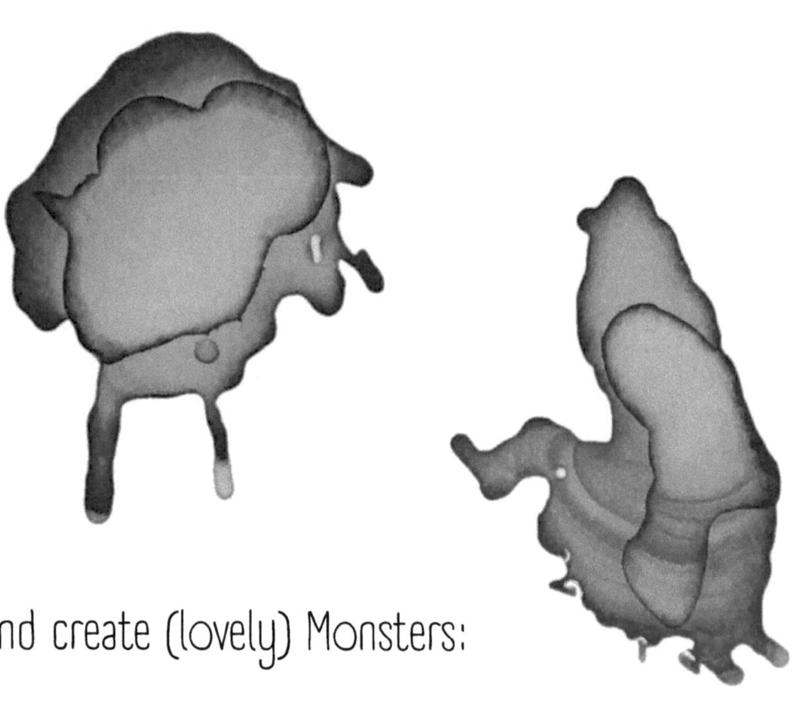

Add lines and create (lovely) Monsters:

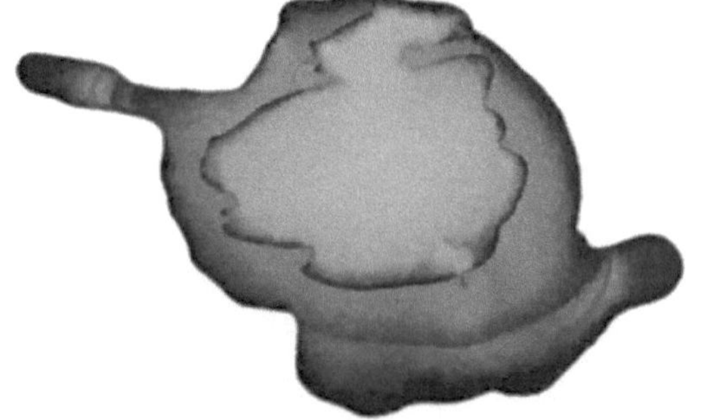

Check also out the other Books by @hannasroth:

"Kreatives-Fantasie-
Tier-ABC-Malbuch"

Check also out the other Books by @hannasroth:

"Kreatives Blumen-ABC-Malbuch"

Check also out the other Books by @hannasroth:

"WRITING BAD WORDS…"

SPACE
FOR YOUR
OWN
WISDOM

IF THEY
GHOST,
THEY'RE
TOAST.

IF THEY
DELAY,
LET THEM
FADE
AWAY

SOME FLOWERS
BLOOM TO BE
ADMIRED,
NOT PICKED.

QUESTIONS YOUR
CAREER?
SWIPE LEFT MY DEAR!

SWIPING
LEFT ON A
JERK
IS SWIPING
RIGHT FOR
YOUR
SANITY.

SPRINKLE GLITTER
AND MOVE ON

NO SPARK
NO START

A MATCH IN
TEXT,
BUT NONE IN
HEART,
BEST BE
SWIPED
APART.

FEAR OF LOVE IS NAUGHT
BUT A COWARDS EXCUSE

A MATCH IN TEXT,
BUT NONE IN HEART,
BEST BE SWIPED
APART.

IF BE
GHOSTETH, LET
HIM WANDER
IN THE DARK
WOODS - THY
PLACE IS TOO
BRIGHT FOR
HIS SHADOWS

WHEN IN DOUBT, LET YOUR HEART LOG OUT.

IF THEY LOVEBOMB,
CHANNEL YOUR INNER
TAYLOR
AND LET KARMA
HANDLE THE REST.

IF THEY
BREADCRUMB,
LET THEM STAY
DUMB

A HEART
UNMATCHED
IS A
HEART
UNSNATCHED

GHOST THE
TOXICITY
BEFORE IT
HAUNTS YOU

IF HIS WORDS BE
HONEYED BUT HIS
ACTIONS BE STINGS,
CAST HIM FROM
THY GARDEN - THY
HEART DESERVETH
BETTER.

NO SPARK
NO START

KISS A FROG, GET
SLIMY LIES -
FUCK THAT NOISE,
AND DRIE THY
EYES.

IF THEIR
ATTENTION
FADES
LIKE AUTUMN
LEAVES,
FIND JOY IN
WHAT YOUR
HEART
BELIEVES

IF THEY
CATFISH WITH
TALES SO
GRAND, LET
NOT THY
TRUST SHIP
THROUGH THY
HAND.

A KNIGHT
WITHOUT
COURAGE IS NO
MORE THAN A
FOOL WITH A
SWORD.

IN A WORLD OF
FROGS,
I'M A FUCKING
UNICORN!

DATE
SMART
NOT
FAST!

A GARDEN FILLED
WITH PRETTY LIES
MAY FLOURISH
FOR A TIME, BUT
'TIS SURE TO CHOKE
THE HEART THAT
TENDS IT.

NOT EVERY BLOOM
IN THE GARDEN OF
LOVE IS MEANT TO
BE PICKED - SOME
ARE BEST LEFT TO
POISON THE SOIL

IF HIS
PROMISES ARE
AS FLEETING
AS A BREEZE,
LET HIM GO –
THOU
DESERVETH
WINDS THAT
CARRY THEE
TO HAPPINESS

IF THEY
GASLIGHT,
FUCK THEIR
SIGHT!

IF THEY
ARE JUST
FISHING
FOR LIKES,
DON'T GET
CAUGHT

THOU SHALT NOT
SETTLE FOR A
ROGUE WHOSE
GALLANT WORDS
ARE BUT FLEETING
ECHOES IN THE
DIGITAL WIND.

LADIES AND
GENTLEMEN,
CAST NOT THINE
PEARLS
BEFORE SWINE
WHO
DALLY IN SHALLOW
BANTER

IF THEY
GHOST,
THEY'RE
TOAST.

Dating Proverbs:
Ancient Wisdom for Modern Love

totally made up

by

@hannasroth

Hannas
ROTH

Impressum:
Hanna Roth
c/o COCENTER
Koppoldstr. 1
86551 Aichach